FORCES

Nicolas Brasch

NELSON
CENGAGE Learning

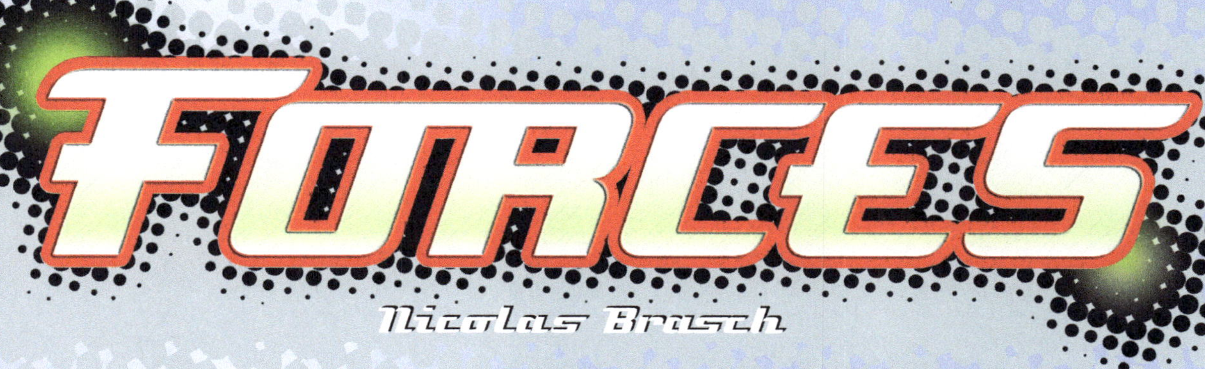

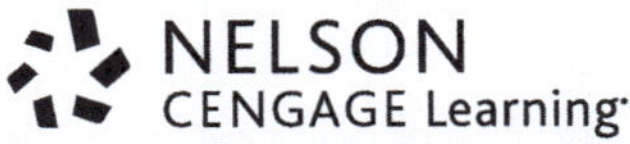

Australia • Brazil • Japan • Korea • Mexico • Singapore • Spain • United Kingdom • United States

Forces

Fast Forward
Silver Level 23

Text: Nicolas Brasch
Illustrations: Mark Wilson
Editor: Cameron Macintosh
Design: James Lowe
Series design: James Lowe
Production controller: Seona Galbally
Photo research: Gilllian Cardinal
Audio recordings: Juliet Hill, Picture Start
Spoken by: Matthew King and Abbe Holmes
Reprint: Siew Han Ong

Acknowledgements
The author and publisher would like to acknowledge permission to reproduce material from the following sources: Front and back covers; Photolibrary/ AAP Image/AFP Photo/Karim Jaafar, p 4 bottom left; Bill Aron/Photo Edit, p 6; Newspix/Patrick Hamilton, p 4 bottom right; Photolibrary, pp 5, 11, 12-17, 20-1, 23. Sport the Library/Robb Cox, p 22; Stock Connection/Alamy, p 19.

ISBN 978 0 17 012703 5
ISBN 978 0 17 012693 9 (set)

Cengage Learning Australia
Level 7, 80 Dorcas Street
South Melbourne, Victoria Australia 3205
Phone: 1300 790 853

Cengage Learning New Zealand
Unit 4B Rosedale Office Park
331 Rosedale Road, Albany, North Shore NZ 0632
Phone: 0508 635 766

For learning solutions, visit cengage.com.au

Printed in Australia by Ligare Pty Ltd
7 8 9 10 11 12 20 19 18 17 16

THE UNIVERSITY OF MELBOURNE

Evaluated in independent research by staff from the Department of Language, Literacy and Arts Education at the University of Melbourne.

Contents

Chapter 1

FORCES

When a weightlifter lifts weights or a cricketer strikes a ball with a bat, they are applying a force.

A force can either be a pull or a push.

Forces make things move.

The weights move because the weightlifter pulls them up.

The ball moves because the cricketer pushes it with the bat.

Forces also make things go faster, slow down, stop or change direction.

Some forces, such as **gravity**, can act over long distances. For example, when a skydiver dives from an aeroplane, he or she is pulled down towards the Earth.

There are many types of forces.

They include magnetic forces, gravitational force, electrostatic force and frictional force.

Chapter 2

MAGNETIC FORCES

Magnets have magnetic forces.
A magnet can draw other objects towards it.
This is called the force of attraction.
A magnet can also push other objects away from it.
This is called the force of repulsion.

the force of repulsion at work between two magnets

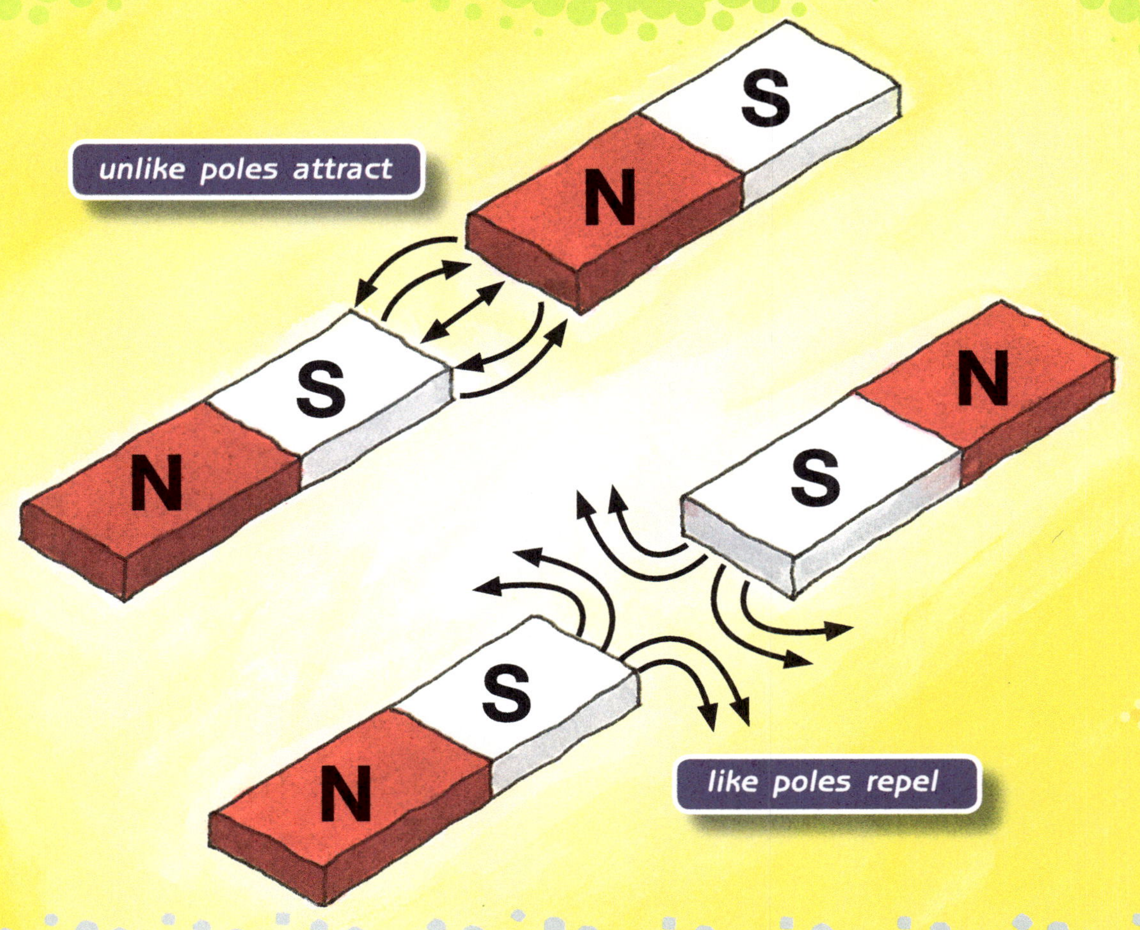

Magnets work in this way because all magnets have two poles.

One pole is called the north pole while the other pole is called the south pole.

When two magnets are put together, unlike poles attract each other and like poles repel each other.

So, the north pole of one magnet will attract the south pole of another magnet.

But two north poles, or two south poles, will repel each other when put together.

Running Words 220

Chapter 3

ELECTROSTATIC FORCE

Electrostatic force was discovered more than 2500 years ago by an ancient Greek called Thales of Miletus.

He found that when he rubbed a piece of **amber** on a piece of sheepskin, bits of dried grass held close to the amber would jump up and stick to the amber. The same thing happened if he held the amber close to feathers.

Many centuries later, in 1600, Dr William Gilbert, an Englishman, found that when he rubbed glass, wax and rubber, things would stick to them, too. What Thales of Miletus and Dr Gilbert had found was electrostatic force, or static electricity.

What Is Static Electricity?

Static electricity is a form of electricity caused by **friction**. Friction occurs when two objects are rubbed together. So, Thales of Miletus caused friction when he rubbed amber with sheepskin.

This friction caused the balance of positive and negative charges to change, and resulted in an electrical charge occurring.

Static electricity does not run in a steady current, but it can leap from one object to another. If people come into contact with static electricity, it can cause their hair to stand on end.

Chapter 4

GRAVITATIONAL FORCE

Because of gravitational force, what goes up must come down.

Gravity affects us every second of the day – it even keeps us on the Earth's surface.

It keeps cups on tables and makes snow fall to the ground.

It keeps water in swimming pools.

What Is Gravity?

Gravity is the force that pulls all objects with **mass** towards each other.

Every object has mass, so every object is pulling on every other object.

However, this doesn't mean that all objects are pulled together into one large blob.

The force of gravity pulls skydivers down to Earth.

The pull of gravity between objects depends on the mass of the objects.
The more mass an object has, the bigger the pull of gravity on it.
The Earth has more mass than a person, for example, so it pulls really hard.
This is why people stay on the ground instead of floating out into space.

Gravity and Space

Gravitational force affects objects on the Earth's surface, keeping them on the ground.
It affects objects in outer space, too.
The Earth's gravitational force pulls objects like space shuttles and satellites into a circular path around itself.

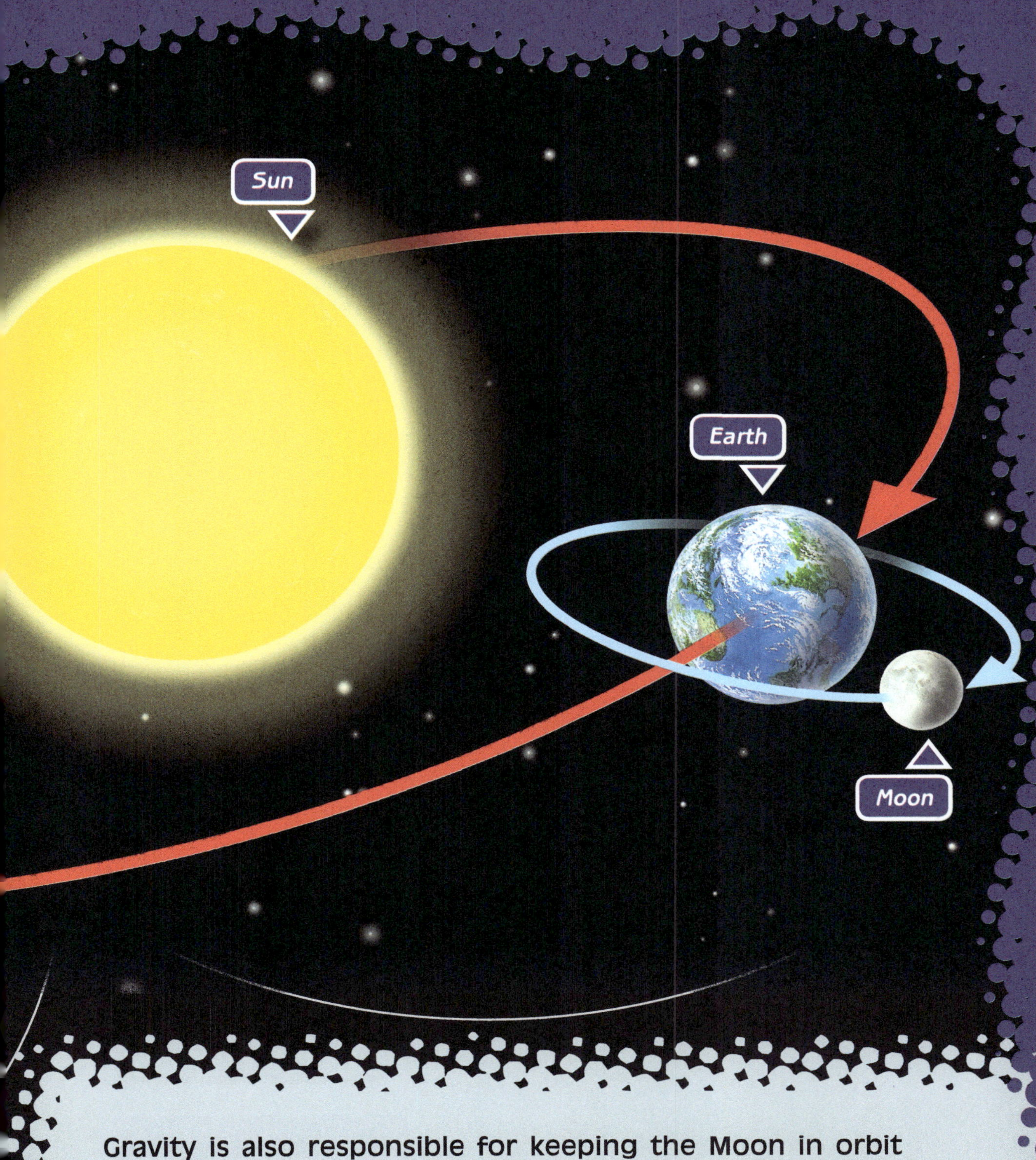

Gravity is also responsible for keeping the Moon in orbit around the Earth, and the Earth itself in orbit around the Sun.

Chapter 5

FRICTIONAL FORCE

When no one catches a ball that has been thrown, gravity pulls the ball down to Earth. But the ball doesn't keep on rolling forever. This is because, after the ball bounces and rolls, frictional force acts on it to make it slow down and stop. Frictional force, or friction, slows or stops objects or keeps them from moving.

Friction helps people to walk, run and climb. The friction between the ground and the bottom of a pair of walking boots helps people to keep their grip on wet or rough ground.

What Is Friction?

Friction occurs when two things rub against each other. It can make things that are moving slow down. So, if a person who is riding a bicycle on flat ground stops pedalling, he or she will start to slow down. Eventually, the bicycle will stop. It is frictional force that is stopping the movement.

Different surfaces can exert different amounts of friction.

A wet or greasy road exerts less friction on rubber tyres than a dry bitumen road.

Reducing Friction

Sometimes, friction needs to be reduced so people and things can move quickly and easily. Swimmers who need to move through the water quickly to win swimming races wear sleek swimsuits and tightly fitting swimming caps to reduce the friction between themselves and the water. Some swimmers shave all the hair from their bodies to reduce friction, too.

In addition, skiers wax their skis to reduce friction between the bottom of their skis and the snow, so they can go downhill faster.

Glossary

amber a yellow-coloured resin

friction the resistance an object encounters when it moves over another object or surface

gravity the force that pulls objects towards each other

mass the amount of material contained in an object

Index